THE
TWELVE DAYS
OF CHRISTMAS

Illustrations
Susan Spellman

Publications International, Ltd.

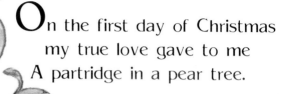

On the first day of Christmas
my true love gave to me
A partridge in a pear tree.

On the second day of Christmas
my true love gave to me
Two turtle doves
And a partridge in
a pear tree.

On the third day of Christmas
my true love gave to me
Three French hens,
Two turtle doves,
And a partridge in
a pear tree.

On the fourth day of Christmas
my true love gave to me
Four calling birds,
Three French hens,
Two turtle doves,
And a partridge in
a pear tree.

On the fifth day of Christmas
    my true love gave to me
Five golden rings,
Four calling birds,
Three French hens,
Two turtle doves,
And a partridge in a pear tree.

On the sixth day of Christmas
my true love gave to me
Six geese a-laying,
Five golden rings,
Four calling birds,
Three French hens,
Two turtle doves,
And a partridge in
a pear tree.

On the seventh day of Christmas
    my true love gave to me
Seven swans a-swimming,
Six geese a-laying,
Five golden rings,
Four calling birds,
Three French hens,
Two turtle doves,
And a partridge in a pear tree.

On the eighth day of Christmas
   my true love gave to me
Eight maids a-milking,
Seven swans a-swimming,
Six geese a-laying,
Five golden rings,
Four calling birds,
Three French hens,
Two turtle doves,
And a partridge in a pear tree.

On the ninth day of Christmas
my true love gave to me
Nine ladies dancing,
Eight maids a-milking,
Seven swans a-swimming,
Six geese a-laying,
Five golden rings,
Four calling birds,
Three French hens,
Two turtle doves,
And a partridge in a pear tree.

On the tenth day of Christmas
   my true love gave to me
Ten lords a-leaping,
Nine ladies dancing,
Eight maids a-milking,
Seven swans a-swimming,
Six geese a-laying,
Five golden rings,
Four calling birds,
Three French hens,
Two turtle doves,
And a partridge in a pear tree.

On the eleventh day of Christmas
    my true love gave to me
Eleven pipers piping,
Ten lords a-leaping,
Nine ladies dancing,
Eight maids a-milking,
Seven swans a-swimming,
Six geese a-laying,
Five golden rings,
Four calling birds,
Three French hens,
Two turtle doves,
And a partridge in a pear tree.

On the twelfth day of Christmas
   my true love gave to me
Twelve drummers drumming,
Eleven pipers piping,
Ten lords a-leaping,
Nine ladies dancing,
Eight maids a-milking,
Seven swans a-swimming,
Six geese a-laying,
Five golden rings,
Four calling birds,
Three French hens,
Two turtle doves,
And a partridge in a pear tree.